LEARN TO PLAY
BLUES

Anthony Marks and Ana Sanderson

History consultant: Howard Rye
Edited by Philippa Wingate
Designed by Andy Griffin and Nicky Morse
Illustrated by Peter Froste and Gerald Wood

Original music by Ana Sanderson
Additional tunes by Anthony Marks

First published in 1995 by Usborne Publishing Ltd, Usborne House, 83-85 Saffron Hill London EC1N 8RT, England.

Contents

About Blues

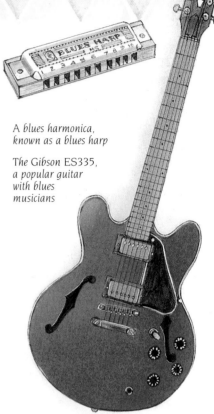

Blues is a style of music that was developed by African Americans at the beginning of the 20th century in the South of the USA. It is now one of the most important musical styles in the world. This book is about the history and development of blues, with tunes to play and ideas for making music.

The word "blues" is not only used to describe a type of music. It is also used to mean a sad or melancholy state of mind. Performers sang blues to express these feelings and emotions. Some blues songs tell of the hard lives led by African Americans, while others tell the stories of important events and people. Others deal with more general subjects like hopes, dreams and love affairs.

The front cover of Jim Jackson's "Kansas City Blues"

About this book

If you are unfamiliar with blues, it might help if you play the tunes on pages 6-9 first. These are four easy pieces that will help you to hear how blues sounds. They will also introduce you to some of the most important aspects of blues playing, and explain how

to get the most out of the music. After that, the book covers the historical development of blues, and gives examples of its various styles.

The pieces on pages 6-9 are very different from each other, but they are all blues music. You can recognize blues tunes in several ways. They are nearly all based on certain chains and patterns of chords. These are called blues progressions, and they are explained on page 19 and elsewhere in the book.

Blues is also recognizable because it is usually played on a few popular instruments: piano, guitar, and harmonica. Most of the pieces in this book are written for piano or keyboard, but many contain parts for guitar, harmonica, and other melody instruments. These may be useful if you want to play music with friends - you can find out more about this on page 63.

You can also often recognize blues because of the way the musicians play their instruments. Most blues musicians make parts of their music up as they go along. This is called improvisation. You can learn more about this on page 19, and find out how to do it on pages 31, 39 and 59.

A blues harmonica, known as a blues harp

The Gibson ES335, a popular guitar with blues musicians

Playing the tunes

There are blues tunes to play throughout the book. As well as telling you something about the different blues styles, each page contains tips about playing the music well. The metronome markings at the start of each piece tell you what speed to play, but you might feel more comfortable with a different speed.

Most of the pieces contain piano fingering numbers. Some of these may feel rather strange if you have not played blues before, but they will help you to play in an authentic blues style. Once you are familiar with the music, however, you may want to try your own fingerings.

At the end of the book, you will find more advice about playing blues, and suggestions about blues music to listen to.

A collection of blues sheet-music, record labels and publicity pictures of blues performers

4

Records and stars

Because blues developed at the same time as sound recording, its history is closely linked with the growth and development of the recording industry. It was one of the first types of music to become popular on the basis of recordings and recording stars. You can read about the history of recording, and of blues records, on pages 24 and 25. Throughout the book there is also information about the life and music of many of the most famous blues musicians.

The early part of the book explains the origins of blues. It traces the development of the style, from its beginnings in certain types of African, American and European music to the appearance of the first blues tunes. Later on, you can find out about the different types of blues that developed all over America as the music became more popular.

Eventually blues became the basis of much of today's popular music, especially jazz and rock. Towards the end of the book, you can find out about the influence of blues on these later styles, and about blues musicians today.

The home of the blues

This map shows the states which make up the United States of America. It includes the main towns and cities mentioned in this book. Blues originated in the Southern states of Mississippi, Texas and Louisiana and gradually spread elsewhere.

This globe shows where the United States of America are situated

A map of the United States of America

Blue Melody

Blues scales and blue notes

By the 19th century, most American and European music was based on major and minor scales. But in parts of Africa, a lot of music was based on other scales. Some had fewer notes, and some scales contained notes that were slightly lower or higher than in American or European music. This affected blues, which developed among Africans in America. It is one reason why blues sounds different from other music.

To hear the difference, play a C major scale, followed by the main notes of a blues scale.

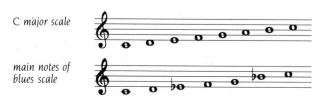

Blues musicians also play some individual notes of the blues scale differently. For example, in the blues scale you have just played, they might make the E flat and B flat sound a bit higher, nearer to E and B. Notes like this are called blue notes. They make the music sound as if it is "between" major and minor keys. This may be why blues music feels sad or "blue".

Because there is no note on the piano between E flat and E, it is easiest to hear the effect of blue notes if you sing them. Play the blues scale again, and sing each note. Make the E flat and B flat a bit higher (play E flat and E, then try to sing between the two notes). You can do this on a guitar too, by "bending" the strings (see page 35). To find out how to imitate blue notes on a piano, see page 28.

Blues rhythms

When playing blues, it is very important to keep a steady rhythm. This piece will help you to practise this. Try learning the left-hand part first, making sure you play the crotchet rhythm very evenly. Once you can do this, add the right hand notes over the top, counting carefully. Try not to speed up or slow down.

In a blues band, the rhythm is usually kept steady by the drummer and bass player. In *Walking Blues*, the left hand part imitates the steady pulse of a double bass player, which is known as a walking bass. If you play the left hand of *Walking Blues* very evenly, the quaver rhythms in the right will be easier to play.

Busy Blues

Syncopation

In *Busy Blues*, you have to play some of the notes on unusual beats of the bar. This is called syncopation. Syncopation is an important part of blues, because it makes the music very rhythmic and energetic. It needs practice, but it will become easier once you are familiar with how it sounds. Try these playing hints:

Learn the left-hand part, then fit the right hand over the top. Work out the rhythms carefully, especially the rests and tied notes. Play evenly, without rushing or forcing the rhythm. Listen carefully to the syncopations, so that you learn how they sound. The more you play *Busy Blues*, the easier it will become.

Lazy Day Blues

Triplets

In *Lazy Day Blues*, you have to play three quavers in the space of two. The figure 3 above the first two groups of quavers tells you to do this. The sign *sim.* over the third group means you continue to play triplet quavers throughout the piece. Many blues tunes have a triplet rhythm. Triplets make slow pieces like this one feel relaxed, but they can also add urgency to faster tunes.

Many blues musicians make the first quaver of a triplet group a little longer and louder than the others. Often they also shorten (or "clip") the last one in the group. This creates a very expressive, "rolling" rhythm.

You could try this with *Lazy Day Blues*, once you can play it. But make sure that you always keep the left hand crotchet beats absolutely regular.

The Origins of Blues

From the 17th century onwards, millions of Africans were taken by force to the Southern states of America. They were sold as slaves, mainly to the owners of cotton plantations. Blues developed in the 19th century, among slaves and their descendants.

The African slave trade

Slaves were taken from many countries in Africa. When they reached the United States of America, families were often split up and sent to different parts of the country. This was largely because slave owners wanted to make it difficult for them to organize revolts. As a result, slaves in each area had different cultures, languages and religions, and were forced to adopt the English language and Christian religion of their owners.

An advertisement offering money for slaves

A plan of how African slaves were packed into the cargo deck of a slave trader's ship

Slaves were not usually allowed to organize their own social events. But they often made music to accompany themselves while they were working, or for religious purposes. This music formed the basis of the blues. It was influenced by the styles of music of their homeland, Africa, and also by the music the slaves had heard in America.

A new freedom

In 1820 a law was passed banning the slave trade. No more slaves were brought to America. Gradually slaves were set free. By 1850 there were over a million freed slaves in America. They set up their own communities, churches, and schools. In 1865, after the end of the American Civil War, slavery was outlawed altogether. As the population of liberated slaves grew, so did the demand for music, dancing and other forms of entertainment. Gradually, blues evolved from the different types of music that slaves had used. The most important of these were religious music, work songs and hollers. (There are examples of these styles on the next four pages, and you find out more about them below. There is more about the entertainment music of freed slaves on pages 16 and 17.)

Religious music

Slaves were encouraged to adopt the Christian religion. Often, however, they were not allowed to attend church with slave-owners, so they developed their own forms of worship.

Sometimes they used the prayers and songs of white American Protestants, but more often they invented their own. One of their most popular methods of prayer was known as call-and-response. This was probably based on similar types of song that originated in Africa.

Some of these styles of music are still found in parts of Africa today.

African musicians today: this man is playing a drum made from the skin of a fruit called a gourd.

This instrument, called a balafon, is a type of xylophone. The player hits the strips of wood with beaters.

The ring-shout, a popular form of worship and dance among African Americans, originated in West Africa.

In call-and-response prayers, the preacher sang sections of a tune, and the congregation sang a reply. In the 19th century, this was often done to accompany a dance called a ring-shout, which also originated in Africa. A group of singers stood in a circle, then moved round, singing and clapping in time to the music.

The Fisk Jubilee Singers, a popular 19th-century spiritual choir

As freed slaves set up their own churches, they organized choirs to sing their own religious music. By the late 19th century, there were thousands of choirs, and a new type of religious song, the spiritual, had become popular with African Americans.

Some spiritual choirs became very well-known, and many blues performers had their first contact with music through church choirs. Some blues musicians, especially those in country areas, included a selection of religious songs in their performances.

Work songs

People have always used music, songs and chants to make their work less boring and to keep in time with each other. Slaves and other workers developed special rhythmic chants called work songs to coordinate their actions during the hard, physical work that they had to do. These tasks included felling trees and wood-chopping, laying tracks on the railroad, dock-work, crop-picking and breaking rocks. There were different songs to suit the actions of each type of job.

Work songs usually had strong rhythms and were often based on call-and-response patterns. The leader of a

19th-century workers laying railroad tracks

work party called out a command, and the workers shouted or sang a reply in rhythm. This helped them to keep in time with each other as they worked.

Convicts from a prison camp breaking rocks

Hollers

"Holler" is American slang for "shout". Hollers were not complete songs, but short fragments of words and music. In country areas, workers sang their hollers alone as they worked, or while walking home from the fields. Some workers also used hollers to call to each other, sending messages from one field to the next.

Many singers could be recognized by their distinctive hollers, which they made personal by using special singing techniques. These included yodelling (alternating rapidly between high and low notes), falsetto (high-pitched singing), and glissandi (sliding). These calls are forerunners of the very personal styles of later blues performers. Like early field workers, many blues singers are instantly recognizable by the way they sing or play.

A boy bringing refreshment to people working in the fields

The Promised Land

$\quad \bullet = 92$

Oh _____ Lord _____ show me the way to the pro-mised land._

Oh _____ Lord _____ show me the way to the pro-mised land._

Look to-wards Jor-dan tell me what do you see?_ A gold-en char-i-ot a-com-ing for me.

Oh _____ Lord _____ show me the way to the pro-mised land._

Slaves and freedom

"The promised land" is a common phrase in spirituals. Most spirituals were based on bible stories. The Jewish people's release from slavery in Egypt was a popular theme. For them, the promised land was Israel. For African slaves, the phrase had two meanings. It referred to the idea of heaven, and to the possibility of being freed from slavery on Earth too.

Playing this tune

The Promised Land is a call-and-response song (see page 10). The first two bars of each line would be sung by a preacher. The next two bars are the congregation's response. When you can play this tune, try singing it, on your own or with friends.

To get the effect of call-and-response, play or sing the preacher's part loudly. Then make the congregation's reply part quieter.

About this tune

Because *On my Way Home* is a holler (see page 11), it would have had no accompaniment. You can sing it, play it on a melody instrument, or use one hand on the piano. Take care with the rhythms.

Recording the past

Today, workers no longer sing hollers. However we know what they sounded like from early recordings of field workers. These were made in Mississippi in the 1940s by American folk-song researchers.

Follow the Leader

Working in rhythm ▽ ▽ ▽

Some work songs, like the one opposite, had quite slow rhythms. They were meant to help workers lift heavy axes or hammers between the main beats. Others, like *Follow the Leader*, were faster. Slaves sang them to entertain themselves while they worked, and to make their jobs less boring. The common feature of all work songs is their strong, energetic beat, which later became one of the most important parts of the blues style.

Playing this tune ▽ ▽ ▽

Try playing *Follow the Leader* as a duet, with a melody instrument like a violin playing the top line. Or play it as a piano solo - as the top line hardly overlaps with the bottom two, it can be played without leaving any notes out. Or, to get the proper call-and-response effect, play just the top and bottom lines. To make the rhythms sound energetic, play the repeated Ds in bars 2, 4, 6 and 8 with a slight accent.

Woodchopper's Work Song

Work songs ▽ ▽ ▽ ▽

This is a work song, and would have been sung by a leader and a chorus. Play it on the piano first, and when you are familiar with the tune, sing the words. *Woodchopper's Work Song* will sound most effective if it is sung by a group. Pick a leader to sing the opening phrase, and get the others to sing the chorus: "Just choppin' wood". Clap, stamp, or bang a tambourine or drum, wherever you see the word "CHOP!". This will help you keep in rhythm.

Recording the past ▽ ▽ ▽

Like hollers, work songs slowly died out in the first half of the 20th century, mainly because most of the traditional labouring jobs were taken over by machines. By the 1940s, they only survived among Black inmates of prison camps. These people were forced to do hard physical work as a punishment. Many work songs were recorded in prisons by musicologists (people who study the history and development of music), as late as the 1960s.

The First Blues

In the late 19th century, the forerunners of blues began to reach the general public through various kinds of entertainments and shows. You can find out more about these below. Pages 18-23 show examples of the different types of music that show performers played and made popular.

Minstrel shows

Minstrel shows became very popular in the second half of the 19th century. Minstrel groups performed the traditional songs and dances of plantation slaves at theatres and concert halls all over the country. These shows often contained comic sketches and other acts too.

This picture of a minstrel group called the Ethiopian Serenaders was taken from a copy of their sheet-music, published in 1847.

The first minstrel performers were white, but after the Civil War, African Americans began to form their own minstrel groups. They became very successful all over the United States of America. Many early blues musicians, including W. C. Handy (see Star File), sang minstrel songs and took part in minstrel shows.

The sheet-music for W.C. Handy's minstrel hit "Joe Turner Blues" and "Dixie's Land" written for Bryant Minstrels

Minstrel hits

The first successful minstrel tune was *Jump Jim Crow*, by Thomas D. Rice. It was based on a song he had heard in the late 1820s.

This illustration was taken from the cover of a sheet-music edition of Thomas D. Rice's "Jump Jim Crow".

The earliest known recordings of African American music by African Americans are of minstrel banjo playing by James and George Bohee, made in London about 1890. No copies of these records have yet been found, but we know about them from advertisements. By the end of the 19th century, huge sales of the sheet music for minstrel tunes demonstrated the style's popularity.

Songsters

As well as minstrel songs, early blues singers performed material from many different musical traditions. Black singers in rural areas often adapted folk and cowboy songs as well as old ballads that they learned from immigrants who had come to America from Europe. These singers were known as songsters.

One of the most famous songsters was Huddie Ledbetter, who became known as Leadbelly (see Star File). He is said to have known more than 500 songs.

Songsters' ballads

Many songster ballads were drawn from European folk songs. *The Unfortunate Rake*, a British ballad about a dying soldier, became an American cowboy song, *The Dying Cowboy*. Later it became a blues song about a dying gambler, called *St. James's Infirmary Blues*.

Some ballads told of heroes, real and legendary. *Casey Jones* is based on the life of a real train driver. He died on April 29, 1900 in Mississippi, when the train he was driving collided with a freight train. Ordering his black fireman, Sim Webb, to jump from the cab, Jones stayed on board to apply the train's brakes right up to the moment of impact.

The ballad *John Henry, the Steel-Drivin' Man*, which tells the story of a fatal battle between a steel-driver and a machine, may be based on an actual worker on the Chesapeake and Ohio railroad in West Virginia in the 1870s.

Railroad ballads were often performed by songsters.

Ballads were not only about heroes and heroines. One song tells of a gambler called Stack O'Lee, who shot and killed an opponent, Billy Lyons. The ballad *Frankie and Johnnie* is thought to have been inspired by a woman named Frankie Baker, who murdered her lover, Albert Britt in St. Louis in October 1899.

The sheet-music for "Stack O'Lee" by Furry Lewis, a typical songster's ballad

Tent shows

Besides songsters, other performers helped to popularize early blues in the American South. Tent shows moved from town to town, setting up in marquees for a few nights in each place. The most famous tent show was Silas Green's Rabbit Foot Minstrels, from New Orleans.

Many tent show performers were women who sang about life and its problems. They were often accompanied by small bands of musicians. Ida Cox (see Star File) was a well-known tent show singer.

A poster advertising the Rabbit Foot Minstrels, a touring show

Medicine shows

After the American Civil War, many doctors toured the country. They brought with them special medicines of their own invention, which they claimed could cure a wide range of ills. To attract and entertain customers, they organized shows. Many early blues singers took part in these medicine shows.

Crowds gather around a doctor's wagon to watch the free entertainment.

IDA COX

Blues singer Ida Cox (1896-1967) joined a minstrel show as a child, and was singing in theatres by the age of 14. With her nasal, resonant singing style, she performed in a very traditional style.

She composed many of her own songs including *Ida Cox's Lawdy Lawdy Blues* and *I've Got the Blues for Rampart Street*. She is considered by many to be one of the finest ever female blues singers.

W. C. HANDY

Blues composer W. C. Handy (William Christopher Handy, 1873-1958), is known as the Father of the Blues. He began his career as a cornet soloist touring with Mahara's Minstrels. Later he led a band in Mississippi, playing ragtime (see page 22) and minstrel music.

He published many songs, including *Memphis Blues* (1912) and *St. Louis Blues* (1914), which were the first widely successful blues tunes.

LEADBELLY

Leadbelly (Huddie Ledbetter, 1889-1949) was a guitarist and singer. By the age of 15 he was a famous musician in Louisiana, but in 1918 he was sent to prison for murder.

In the 1930s, John Lomax, a collector of folk songs, discovered Leadbelly in jail. He arranged for Leadbelly to be released and began recording songs, including *Honey I'm All Out and Down* (1935) and *Goodnight Irene* (1943).

The Happy Minstrel

♩ = 100-108

The minstrel tradition

In the late 1860s, African American singers and
dancers began forming their own minstrel groups.
These quickly became more popular than the
earlier white minstrel performers. They performed
plays and comic sketches based on plantation life,
and often used religious music as well as songs
and dance tunes. By the 1890s, black minstrel
shows had become popular all over America.

Minstrel tunes

The early white minstrels based their songs on
simple European dance tunes of the 18th century.
Later, black minstrels added African American
rhythms and made the melodies more elaborate.
Sometimes they also added call-and-response
sections (see page 10) like the ones in this tune.
Play *The Happy Minstrel* gently, but make sure you
keep the syncopated rhythms strictly in time.

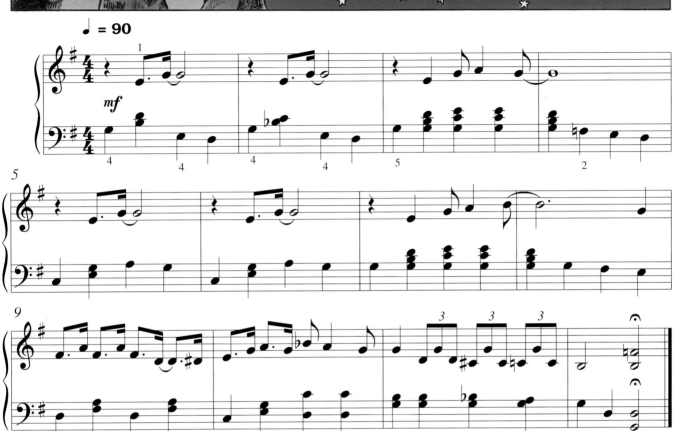

The first blues songs

The style we now call blues developed in the first decade of the 20th century among tent-show singers, songsters and minstrels.

Most of these people did not read music, so they made up words and tunes as they went along. This is called improvisation. As the starting point of blues improvisation, musicians used standard patterns of chords and rhythms, called blues progressions. These progressions were well-known by 1910, but may have existed long before this.

How blues progressions work

Hound Dog Blues uses a progression known as a 12-bar blues. It is a pattern of chords based on the first, fourth and fifth notes of a major scale, lasting twelve bars. Below you can see these chords on the scale of G major, shown by the Roman numerals I, IV and V.

Blues progressions can be played in any key, but they are always based on the chords built on the first, fourth and fifth notes of a scale. The 12-bar progression repeats chords I, IV and V, one chord per bar, in a strict order, over twelve bars. Below you can see how this works in G major (the chord numbers are shown in brackets after each note).

bars 1-4:	G (I)	C (IV)	G (I)	G (I)
bars 5-8:	C (IV)	C (IV)	G (I)	G (I)
bars 9-12:	D (V)	C (IV)	G (I)	G (I)

Many blues tunes, including Hound Dog Blues, use this pattern, or others similar to it. But no two blues tunes sound alike. Each musician uses the pattern as the starting point for improvisation, adding the features described on pages 6-9: blue notes, syncopations, and more complex chords based on blues scales. Later in the book there is more about this, and about how to improvise.

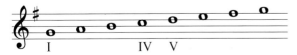

Songster's Tune

Recording the past ▽ ▽ ▽ ▽

ngsters were some of the first popular
sicians to be recorded. Recordings from the
by some of the older musicians, such as
Thomas, show us how songster tunes would
nded in the late 19th century. Thomas
his version of *John Henry the Steel-drivin'*
, playing both guitar and reed pipes.

Like minstrels, many early songsters played banjo.
But slowly the guitar became more common, and
it remained popular among blues musicians. Like
minstrels, some early songsters were accompanied
by other musicians. But like many blues singers,
most songsters performed alone to their own
guitar accompaniment.

Playing this tune

Try *Songster's Tune* on the piano first. Count very carefully, taking care not to rush the syncopations. When you are familiar with it, you could ask someone with a melody instrument, especially a violin, to play the top line.

From ballads to blues

Many songsters' ballads originated in Europe. They were often very simple folk tunes with basic harmonies. They were also rhythmically quite straightforward, as they were often based on the rhythms of European folk dances. The first page of *Songster's Tune* is typical of an early songster ballad with European origins.

Songsters added African American features to the ballads. They used syncopation, flattened notes from the blues scale (see page 6), and highly ornamented vocal lines. This gave ballads a new character, making them one of the most direct forerunners of blues. You can hear this on the second page of *Songster's Tune*.

Dime Rag

♩ = 78

Rags and ragtime

Another forerunner of blues, ragtime was a dance music based on the syncopated ("ragged") rhythms of African American music. It developed at the very end of the 19th century, mainly out of the dances and marches written for minstrel shows. Unlike songsters' ballads and other popular music styles of the period, ragtime pieces were often written by trained composers.

In ragtime, the irregular syncopations of African American music were gradually "smoothed out" into a few standard rhythmic patterns. The most common of these appears throughout *Dime Rag*, and first appears in bars 5 and 6.

Today, ragtime is usually thought of as a style of piano music, but there were also rags for bands and orchestras, and many ragtime songs.

Playing Dime Rag

Try playing the left hand on its own a few times until you can get the quaver beats steady and even. Then add in the right hand, counting the syncopations carefully. Play smoothly, and don't be tempted to rush.

Ragtime first reached the general public at the World's Columbian Exposition, a trade fair that took place in Chicago in 1893. Over 20 million people visited the event, and were able to hear the music for the first time. It rapidly became popular throughout the country. There were a number of famous rag composers, including Ben Harney, Scott Joplin and James Scott.

The huge popularity of ragtime helped early blues to reach a wider audience. W. C. Handy's *Memphis Blues*, published in 1912 with the subtitle "A Southern Rag", was one of the first genuine blues tunes to become successful all over America. Ragtime was going out of fashion by the start of World War I, but by this time blues was an established style of popular music.

Recording the Blues

The man responsible for the first blues recordings was pianist and composer Perry Bradford. In 1920 he convinced the OKeh recording company that there was a large market for blues records. Other companies soon followed OKeh's example.

The first blues records were made by large organizations, such as Paramount, Victor and OKeh.

Recording artists

Most early blues recordings were made by musicians who worked in revues and tent shows. Some record companies simply waited for talented people to arrive at their studios, searching for an opportunity to record. Others paid local agents to listen to potential performers and then sent mobile recording units to record them. The agents appointed by record companies were usually white businessmen, particularly local record dealers who knew what kind of music their black customers liked.

Some agents became expert talent scouts. Henry Spiers, a music-store owner in Jackson, Mississippi, was responsible for recording three of the greatest Mississippi blues performers: Son House, Skip James, and Charley Patton.

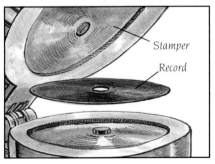

Agents often found talented performers playing on street corners.

Established performers also played a part in bringing new artists to the studios. Some, such as guitarist Lonnie Johnson, actually worked as talent scouts themselves.

A growing industry

In the early 1920s, new blues records were issued at a rate of about one a week. Few people had radios, so buying records was the easiest way to hear new blues songs. The earliest blues recordings were made using a process known as acoustic recording.

To make an acoustic recording, performers played or sang into a large horn. This caused the air inside the horn to vibrate.

The horn was connected to a device called a cutting stylus. The vibrating air made the stylus cut a groove in a disc made of a resin called shellac.

The groove corresponded to the sounds made by the performers.

This "master" disc, was used to produce "stampers", from which individual copies were pressed.

Stamper

Record

In the mid-1920s, the acoustic system was replaced by electrical recording, which was clearer and truer to the original performance.

Race records

Many companies made records specially for the African American market. These were known as "race records" (black Africans at that time often referred to themselves as "the Race"). They were marketed wherever there was a large African American population, usually through local record stores, newspapers and magazines.

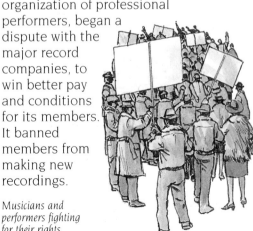

Blues records were sold by mail order through catalogues.

Blues formed a large part of the race record catalogues, especially the music of rural musicians like Sylvester Weaver and Papa Charlie Jackson. But race records were also made by theatre and revue performers, jazz musicians, and religious preachers and singers.

New record companies

In 1942, the American Federation of Musicians, America's largest organization of professional performers, began a dispute with the major record companies, to win better pay and conditions for its members. It banned members from making new recordings.

Musicians and performers fighting for their rights

In addition to this, during the Second World War there was a shortage of shellac. The record companies used their stocks to press records by their best-selling artists. Very few of these performers were blues musicians, so blues began to be neglected by many larger record companies. As a result of these two factors, new, independent companies appeared in the mid-1940s, specializing in recording blues artists.

Chess, Chance and Vee-Jay were among the new independent record labels.

While some established artists like Sonny Boy Williamson, Big Bill Broonzy and Memphis Minnie continued to work for the major companies, many younger performers began recording for the new ones. By the 1950s, labels such as Chess, Vee-Jay, and Savoy dominated the blues market, and many people still associate them with the finest blues recordings.

Blues recording today

In the 1950s and 1960s, the audience for blues continued to change (see page 62). Its original audience in America declined, but blues became popular elsewhere. Independent companies took advantage of the new audiences, investing in blues recording when most of the larger companies would not. Many independent companies still survive, continuing to find new artists and promote their work.

MAMIE SMITH

In 1920, Perry Bradford wrote two songs: *That Thing Called Love* and *You Can't Keep a Good Man Down*. He persuaded OKeh to allow a popular blues singer, Mamie Smith (1883-1946) to record them. The records attracted a lot of attention in the black community. Her second record, *Crazy Blues* and *It's Right Here For You* (1920) was the first ever blues hit, selling 100,000 copies in a month.

MA RAINEY

Ma Rainey (1886-1939) is known as the "Mother of the Blues". Born Gertrude Pridgett in Columbus, Georgia, she appeared in the *Bunch of Blackberries Talent Show* at the age of 12. She became a blues, jazz and vaudeville singer, touring with the Rabbit Foot Minstrels and then with her own Georgia Jazz Band.

Ma Rainey made more than 100 recordings for the Paramount company. Today, her best remembered songs are probably *See See Rider* (1924) and *Soon this Morning* (1927).

BESSIE SMITH

Bessie Smith, known as the "Empress of the Blues" (1894-1937), was probably the most famous female blues singer of all. Born in Chattanooga, Tennessee, she began her career singing in the same shows as Ma Rainey. By the early 1920s, however, she was the star of her own shows, and toured all over America.

Her first recording, *Downhearted Blues* (1923) was an immediate hit. Her other hits include *J.C. Holmes Blues* (1925) and *Young Woman's Blues* (1926).

Swinging Blues for Two

♩ = 92

Playing this tune

Swinging Blues for Two is a duet for a melody instrument (such as the recorder, flute or violin) and piano. You can also perform it as a piano solo, playing the top and bottom lines from bar 5. During the top-line rests in bars 11 and 12, you could fill in the gaps by playing the chords on the middle line.

Gracefully Blue

Blue notes on a piano

Blues pianists could not alter the pitches on a piano to play blue notes, but they developed ways of imitating the pitch bends of guitarists and singers. They did this by playing two notes a semitone apart and "crushing" them together. As the blues piano style developed in the 1920s, crushed notes quickly became one of its most important features. There are notes like this in *Gracefully Blue*, shown as small note-heads.

Playing crushed notes

There are two ways to play crushed notes. First, try sounding the small note slightly before the main note that follows it. Then try overlapping the small note with the main one, so that you hear them together. In quiet tunes like *Gracefully Blue*, the overlap should be short. But in energetic tunes, playing the two notes together for the entire beat makes the music more powerful. Try this in bars 4 and 8 of *Twelve-bar Stride* on the opposite page.

Twelve-bar Stride

Stride piano

This tune is in a style known as stride, which developed in Harlem, New York, around 1910, and reached the peak of its popularity in the 1920s. It is similar to ragtime, but is faster and has more energetic syncopations. The most striking feature of stride piano is the elaborate bass line, which has wide leaps and deep, emphatic bass notes in the left hand.

Playing a stride bass

Practise the left hand slowly, getting used to the large leaps. (It can help to "chop" the lowest note with the side of your fifth finger, but don't hit the keys too hard.) Then add the right hand. Try to play the tune a little faster each time, making sure you keep the rhythm solid. Don't stop if you miss the leaps - keep playing to the end, then go back and practise any bits you find difficult.

Four Hands Blues

Part B

A blues duet ▽ ▽ ▽ ▽ ▽

This tune is a duet for two pianists to play at one piano. It will be easier to learn if both players practise both parts. This will make each person familiar with what the other has to play. Part A is the higher part, for the player on the right. Part B is the lower part, for the player on the left. To help you keep in time, count a few bars of 4/4 together at the correct speed before you start to play.

Part B should be steady and solid, with a clear, firm bassline. Give the syncopated chords in bars 2 and 14 a slight accent to add a "kick". In part A, try playing the dotted quavers and semiquavers as if they were triplet quavers. Split the crotchet beat into three instead of four, and play the semiquaver on the third count. This makes the music sound relaxed and energetic at the same time.

Four Hands Blues

Part A

More about improvising

Four Hands Blues is a classic twelve-bar tune. The first-time bars contain a "turnaround", a phrase that leads back to the start of the progression. This means you can play the 12-bar section between the repeat signs as often as you like. If you do this, the person playing part A could try to improvise (make up a new solo part). On the right are a few tips to help you do this.

The right-hand phrases in bars 5, 6, 9 and 10 are called "fills". They link the main sections of the tune. Try improvising your own fills. At first you could alter the rhythms of the written fills, or change some of the notes. Listen carefully to the result. As you become familiar with the effects of changing the notes and rhythms, you will become more confident about improvising.

Blues Instruments

Blues performers used a variety of musical instruments. Some of these were traditionally popular among folk musicians, while others were homemade for a particular purpose. On page 48 you can find out about the piano, which was also popular with blues players.

Guitars

Guitars are among the most popular blues instruments. Easily portable and reasonably cheap to buy, guitars originated in Mexico and were introduced to the USA by Mexican workers.

This type of guitar, a Gibson ES335 has been played by many blues musicians, like Chuck Berry.

Blues musicians used guitars to produce a variety of sounds. A knife blade drawn along the strings produced a whining sound. This was probably inspired by a type of guitar called the Hawaiian guitar.

A Hawiian guitar is played flat across the knees with a metal tube called a slide.

Guitarists also used the neck of a bottle or a piece of metal tube, often worn on one finger, to produce this effect. "Bottleneck" or slide playing became a widespread technique among blues guitarists.

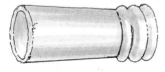
A bottleneck

A metal slide

Amplified blues

Electric guitars became available in the 1930s. They were plugged into amplifiers to make them louder. Many blues musicians played in noisy clubs, so electric guitars quickly became important to them.

Mandolins and banjos

Mandolins have a quiet, delicate sound. They have eight strings.

Banjos have a body made from a piece of skin or plastic stretched over a metal frame. They usually have a wooden back to make the sound louder.

Mandolins, which originally came from Italy, were often used by both early blues players and Southern string bands.

The banjo, an instrument of African origin, was popular with minstrels and string bands.

Violins

Violins were mostly used in groups called string bands, which were popular in the south and east of the USA. They mainly played folk and European dance music, and gradually began to perform ragtime, the music from minstrel shows and other material with African American influences. Some performers, such as Lonnie Johnson, used a violin to accompany blues singers.

A modern violin

Harmonicas

Some blues bands used harmonicas, known as blues harps. A harmonica has the same range as a violin, but is cheaper, more portable and easier to learn.

A harmonica is a small, narrow metal box with metal reeds inside it.

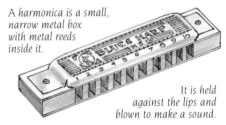

It is held against the lips and blown to make a sound.

Homemade instruments

Many blues musicians, especially those in poor rural areas, made their own instruments from a selection of everyday objects.

A strip of soft metal could be turned into an instrument called a Jew's harp.

Singers could make a buzzing sound by humming through a piece of tissue paper stretched over a comb.

Bones and spoons were beaten together to make a percussive sound.

A washboard was a wooden frame with metal ridges, used to rub clothes. But by tapping the ridges while wearing thimbles, musicians could make a rattling, rhythmic sound.

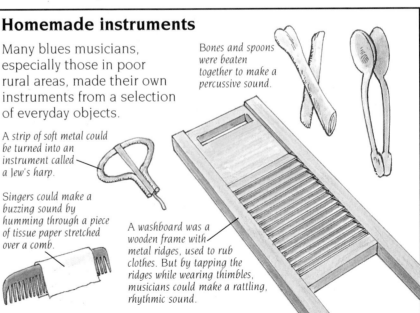

Jug bands

In the 1920s, groups called jug bands became popular. They played homemade instruments, including the large earthenware jugs that contained beer or wine.

A poster advertising the Memphis Jug Band

There were two main groups of jug bands: those based around Memphis, Tennessee and those in Louisville, Kentucky. In Memphis, the bands were fairly primitive, but the Louisville bands were often more sophisticated. Both groups were strongly influenced by minstrels and employed jazz players and other musicians. They included blues tunes, waltzes, music hall songs and popular songs in their performances.

One members of this jug band is playing a homemade double bass.

Jugs

CHARLEY PATTON

Charley Patton (1887-1934) worked around Dockery's plantation near Clarkesville, Tennessee, and hated the discipline of plantation life.

Patton had a gruff, unpolished singing voice. He used a bottleneck, sometimes playing the guitar across his knees, Hawaiian style. His recordings for the Paramount label included songster tunes like *Frankie and Albert* (1929) and spirituals. His most famous blues song was *Pony Blues* (1929).

MEMPHIS MINNIE

Memphis Minnie (1896-1973) was probably the most important female blues guitarist. She grew up in Memphis, Tennessee, and moved to Chicago in 1928. Her first husband was the guitarist Kansas Joe McCoy, and together they recorded a series of vocal and guitar duets. She later worked with many other Chicago musicians. Her recordings for the Vocalion label included the best-selling *Bumble Bee* (1930) and *Joe Louis Strut* (1935).

SONNY BOY WILLIAMSON

Sonny Boy Williamson (1897-1965) was one of the greatest blues harmonica players. He was born in Mississippi, and was originally known as Rice Miller. When he began to broadcast on the radio in 1941, he borrowed the name Sonny Boy Williamson from another harmonica player.

Williamson was over 50 when he made his first recordings. In 1955 he had a hit with *Don't Start me to Talkin'*, backed by Muddy Waters and his band.

Back Porch Blues

Part B

Playing this tune

Back Porch Blues has parts for up to three players. Part B is the piano part, which can be played on its own. Try not to play the dotted quavers and semiquavers in the left hand too rigidly - think of them more as groups of triplet quavers to get an authentic blues rhythm.

Above the music, there are guitar chords to add to the piano part. You could use several different rhythms for them. Try playing on the second and fourth beats of the bar only, or strum in time to the left hand of the piano. Make sure you change from one chord to the next in the right place.

There are diagrams for the guitar chords in this tune on page 63.

Back Porch Blues

Part A

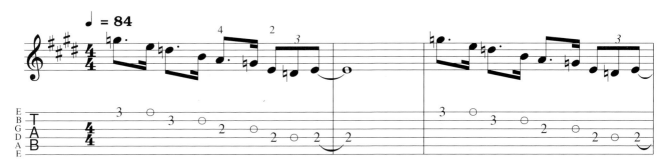

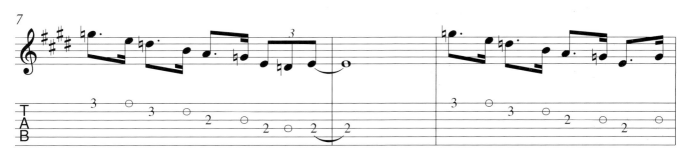

A solo part ▽ ▽ ▽ ▽ ▽

Part A is a solo melody line. You can play it on a flute, violin or recorder, or any other melody instrument. It will also sound very effective on a guitar. The tablature notation on the lower staff may help you to work out which frets to play on each string.

String bending ▽ ▽ ▽ ▽ ▽

If you play the solo part on a guitar, try bending the string each time you play top G. This will help to create an authentic blues sound. Play the note, then gently move the finger holding the string down, pushing the string towards the centre of the guitar neck. The pitch of the note will rise slightly.

35

Up to Five Blues

Playing this tune

Up to five people can play this tune together. Here are some suggestions about how to do this:

As a solo: You can play the piano part on this page on its own. The rhythm should be regular, but put a very slight accent on the first quaver of each pair. This will make them "roll" a little.

When you are familiar with the music, try to play both the top and bottom lines with the left hand only. If you work out the fingering carefully, you can do this for most of the tune. Once you can manage it, try adding the melody line on the opposite page. It may be hard to read from both pages at once, but it will become easier with practice. Alternatively, record the music on this page, either on tape or in the sequencer of an electronic keyboard. Then add the melody line over the top.

As a group: Get a guitarist to strum the chords above the piano part, using this rhythm:

As long as someone plays either the piano or guitar parts on this page, you can add any or all of the parts opposite, on any instruments you like. The melody line opposite could be played with one hand by another pianist. Or ask someone to play it on a melody instrument - harmonica (see opposite), flute, violin, or recorder.

Below the melody there are parts for two rhythm instruments. Use one, such as a drum, for the notes with stems going up, and another, such as a tambourine, for notes with stems going down. Or blow in rhythm over the neck of a large bottle to imitate the sound of a jug band (see page 33).

There are diagrams for the guitar chords in this tune on page 63.

Blues harmonica

Harmonicas can only play in one key, so most blues harmonica (or "harp") players have several instruments, one for each key. Often, instead of using a harmonica in the key of the tune they are playing, they use one in the key a fifth below. This is called playing "cross-harp".

For example, Up to Five Blues is in the key of G, but a blues scale on G contains F natural, which is not available on a harmonica in G. So you have to use a C harmonica, which plays F natural, and play cross-harp. Most "mouth organs" available from toy stores are in C, but a C blues harp bought at a music store will be more reliable.

Playing cross-harp also means that the most important notes of the scale are on the "draw" - you breathe in to play them. Notes on the draw are easier to bend than notes you play by blowing.

Playing this tune on a harmonica

Hold your harmonica so the hole that plays the highest notes is at the right. Most blues harps have ten holes, which may be numbered upwards from left to right. In the music, the numbers above the notes show you which hole to play. The arrow pointing right means "blow"; the arrow pointing left means "draw". So for the first note, you blow through hole 6. For the second, you draw through hole 5.

When you play, put your lips tightly over the holes. This will help you direct the airflow. You can bend the notes on the draw by stopping the hole with your lip or tongue. When you clear the hole after this, the note will bend upwards. Try altering the way you breathe, and experiment with blowing different holes too, to see which makes the melody sound most expressive.

Fishin' Line Blues

The top line

You can play the top line of this tune on any instrument, but a slide guitar would sound best. Use a bottleneck (see page 32). For this tune, you will only need the D and G strings.

Each time you have to repeat the note A, slide up to the note from slightly below it. This will bend the notes slightly, making them more expressive. You can do this with the top C too.

Playing this tune

You can play this as a piano solo by reading the two lowest lines, or add the top line on a melody instrument (see below). The beat of this tune should very relaxed. Clip the last note in each triplet very slightly (see page 9) to get a good rhythm.

More about improvising

If you play the repeated section a few times, the person playing the melody line can improvise a solo part. Base this on the written line, but try adding in other notes and changing the rhythms.

At first, not every note you play will sound good with the accompaniment. It takes time to learn which notes fit best. The more you listen and experiment, the easier improvising becomes.

Country Blues

Once blues was established as an important type of popular music, different styles began to develop in different parts of America. In the 1930s, a style known as country blues became popular. It was based on the music of the earliest blues performers in rural areas, but it became popular throughout America. There were three main centres of country blues: the Mississippi, Texas and the East Coast (see map).

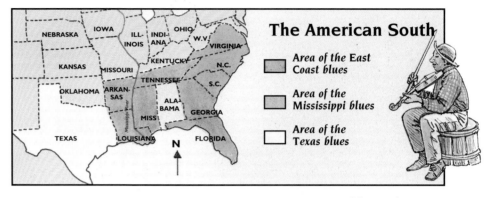

The American South

- Area of the East Coast blues
- Area of the Mississippi blues
- Area of the Texas blues

Mississippi blues

The Mississippi blues style grew up in the Mississippi Valley, especially in the delta of the Yazoo River from Memphis down to Vicksburg. This area is often considered to be the birthplace of blues. The population was mainly made up of black plantation workers. Though these people were no longer slaves, many of them still lived in severe poverty and hardship.

Mississippi blues singers expressed intense emotions, often groaning, humming and even yelling in their songs. Many accompanied themselves with wailing bottleneck guitar playing (see page 32). The main stars of Mississippi blues were Son House, Robert Johnson, Charley Patton and Skip James.

Many country blues players, including Skip James and Charley Patton, began their careers entertaining at rural bars and tenement buildings.

East Coast blues

In the southern states of the Atlantic coast (Florida, Georgia, South Carolina, North Carolina and Virginia), conditions for African Americans were less harsh than in Mississippi or Texas. Many blues artists from this area had a relaxed musical style. They include Blind Blake, Blind Willie McTell, Buddy Moss, Blind Boy Fuller and Brownie McGhee.

A rural duo playing a homemade bass (left) and guitar.

Blind performers have always played an important part in blues music. Unable to do manual work, they turned to music to earn a living. With the enhanced sense of hearing that blind people often have, many became successful musicians.

Some East Coast blues players also performed other music. They appeared with string bands (groups using mainly violins, guitars, and mandolins), and sometimes sang string band tunes as well as blues.

Texas blues

Texas blues was a style that originated in the Southwest of America. Many Texas blues songs are more strongly based on stories than Mississippi blues songs. Subjects included versions of the ballads that had been popular with songsters (see page 16), as well as tales of the hardship and toil of everyday life in rural areas, including famine and drought.

Crop pests like cotton weevils feature in many blues songs.

Texas blues singers often had high, expressive voices, and many of them accompanied themselves on guitar. The best known Texas blues performers include guitarists Blind Lemon Jefferson (see Star File), Lightnin' Hopkins and Texas Alexander.

The Paramount label for one of Blind Lemon Jefferson's hits.

Texas is very close to Mexico, so Texas blues players were very familiar with Mexican music. This influenced the playing of Blind Lemon Jefferson and many others.

The guitar was first played in America by Mexican musicians.

Field recording

The first recordings of country blues performers were made by sound engineers who moved around the country with their recording equipment. This is known as field recording. Some of these people wanted to record music for commercial purposes (see page 24). Others were researchers and historians who were more interested in capturing unusual types of music. Many of the earliest blues styles only survive in recordings made by these field units.

Early sound recording equipment

ROBERT JOHNSON

Robert Johnson (1911-1938) was born in Hazlehurst, Mississippi. In the mid-1930s he recorded many songs with field units in Texas, including *Hellhound on my Trail* (1937), *I Believe I'll Dust my Broom* (1936) and *Ramblin' on my Mind* (1936. He died at the age of 26, probably from poisoned whisky.

Johnson's voice and bottleneck guitar style influenced some important blues singers, notably Elmore James and Muddy Waters.

SON HOUSE

Blues singer Son House (Eddie James, 1902-1988) is thought by many blues experts to be a typical Mississippi blues performer. Only four of his recordings were issued in his lifetime. These include his masterpiece *Preachin' the Blues* (1930), with its half-shouted lyrics and bottleneck guitar playing. The records sold so poorly that a copy of one of them has not yet been found. House was recorded again by the Library of Congress in 1941 and 1942.

BLIND LEMON JEFFERSON

The best known Texas blues performer is Blind Lemon Jefferson (1897-1930). His sight had deteriorated during his childhood and he made a living by singing on the streets of various towns throughout Texas.

With his high, clear voice he made more than 80 records between 1925 and 1929. His best-known songs include *Black Snake Moan* (1927) and *Match Box Blues* (1927). His songs were recorded by many other blues artists.

Mississippi River Blues

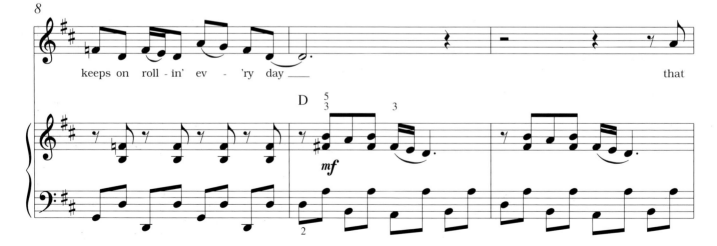

There are diagrams for the guitar chords in this tune on page 63.

Playing this tune

Ask someone to sing or play the top line, or learn to sing it yourself. To accompany it, use the piano part, or the guitar chords, or both. Alternatively, play the tune on the piano alone, reading the top and bottom lines. Add some of the chords from the middle part during the gaps in the top line.

ri-ver was my friend till that day it washed my house a-way___ that

Mis-sis-sip-pi ri - ver came in through my front door___

don't know why you're mad at me but you're no friend of mine a-ny more.

Black Cat Blues

A new kind of bass line

In *Black Cat Blues*, the melody is in the bass line, so play the left hand clearly and firmly. Keep the right-hand chords even and fairly quiet, and fit the syncopated bass part around it. This may feel a bit tricky at first, but it will get easier with practice.

There are diagrams for the guitar chords in this tune on page 63.

Other ways of playing this tune

There are guitar chords above the music, which you could ask someone to strum while you play the left-hand part. Or ask a cellist to play the left-hand part, and accompany it with the right-hand of the piano part or the guitar chords.

Prison Cell Blues

Minor-key blues progressions

Most blues tunes are based on major keys, but blues progressions (see page 19) do exist in minor keys. *Prison Cell Blues* has minor chords in place of the usual major chords on the first and fourth note of the scale.

Playing this tune

Play this piece as a piano solo. Make the crotchet chords firm and steady, but not too loud. Once you are familiar with the tune, you could add the words. Either sing them yourself, or get someone else to sing while you play.

Goin' East Blues

Playing this tune

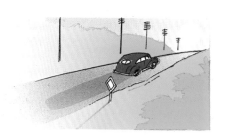

You will already recognize many of the piano blues techniques in *Goin' East Blues*: syncopations, crushed notes and triplet passages. Try not to play too quickly. Practise the wide leaps in the right hand (bars 3, 7 and 11, for example) until you can play them confidently.

Piano Blues

I n the Southern states, where blues originated, pianos were mainly found either in churches or in bars. As a result, piano blues is closely linked to church music and the music that was popular in bars.

Many blues pianists learned to play in Baptist churches, providing gospel music for the congregation.

Barrelhouse piano

Many African Americans worked felling trees in the forests of Texas and Louisiana. After work they went to local bars called barrelhouses. The rough, driving piano style that developed there is known as barrelhouse. Two famous barrelhouse pianists were Will Ezell and Charlie Spand.

To get a loud, forceful sound that could be heard in bars, barrelhouse pianists often put newspaper behind the strings, or metal tacks in the hammers.

Boogie woogie

While barrelhouse developed in rural areas, another style, boogie woogie, was performed in city bars and clubs. Boogie woogie is faster and rhythmically more complex than barrelhouse. It acquired its name from the 1928 recording *Pine Top's Boogie Woogie*, by Clarence "Pine Top" Smith (1904-1929). The style remained popular until the early 1940s; some blues and jazz pianists still play tunes in a boogie woogie style today.

JIMMY YANCEY

Jimmy Yancey (1894-1951) first worked as a tap dancer, but retired from show business in 1925 to become a groundskeeper for the Chicago White Sox, a baseball team.

He developed a serene, melodious version of boogie woogie. He first achieved fame in 1936 when the piano player Meade Lux Lewis recorded his composition *Yancey Special* (1936). After this, Yancey made many recordings, including *Yancey's Bugle Call* (1940).

MEMPHIS SLIM

Born and raised in Memphis, Tennessee, Peter Chapman (1925-1988), known as Memphis Slim, sang and accompanied himself on the piano. His playing was in a rough, powerful style that had its roots in rural barrelhouse music.

At the age of 24 he hitched a ride to Chicago, where he worked as a pianist in Big Bill Broonzy's band. He toured Europe in the 1960s and eventually became a regular performer in Les Trois Maillets, a club in Paris.

Boogie woogie was played at parties that were organized by poor African Americans to raise money to pay their rent.

Crazy Feet Boogie

About boogie woogie

The most important feature of boogie woogie is the bass line, which is an elaborate version of the walking bass (see page 7). Many early boogie bass lines were in even quavers, like the one in this tune. In later boogie woogie tunes, the bass rhythms were often more complicated, like the ones on the next four pages.

Playing this tune

Boogie woogie bass lines can be fairly difficult. Practise this one slowly until you are sure of the notes. Try to "roll" your hand across the octave leaps as smoothly as you can. (If you cannot stretch the octaves, play both quavers on the lower note of each pair.) When you can play the left-hand part confidently try both hands together.

Choo Choo Boogie

Playing this tune

If you play the dotted notes exactly as written, they will sound too rigid. But if you divide the beat into triplets, as on page 30, it will make this tune sound too relaxed. A true boogie woogie rhythm is somewhere in between the two - not too strict, but not too lazy.

A classic boogie bass line

The dotted rhythm left-hand part in this tune is one of the most common boogie bass lines. "Roll" your left hand across the keys, making the bass notes ring out. Practise it slowly at first, then speed up when you are sure of the notes. *Choo choo Boogie* sounds best played at around ♩ = 110, though many boogie players would have shown off their technique by playing it far faster than this.

Special effects

Many boogie tunes contained special effects or "novelty" passages. In *Choo Choo Boogie* there are imitations of the whistles on American freight trains. The sign between the staves in bars 17, 19 and 23 tells you to alternate between the G sharp and the B flat, as quickly as you can, for the whole bar. This tremolo effect, which is often heard in blues piano playing, will need a little practice.

Boogie for Two
Part B

Boogie for Two is a duet for two people at one piano. Play the left hand of Part B an octave lower than written.

Boogie for Two

Part A

See page 51 for an explanation of the sign in bars 1-3, 5, 7, 9 and 11 of this part.

Blues in the City

In the early part of the 20th century, many African Americans moved from rural areas of the South to major cities, mainly in the north and east. As a result, the character of blues changed.

Migration

In the 1890s, 80% of the total African American population lived in the rural areas of the American South. But gradually there were fewer and fewer jobs there. Plantations closed, or became farmed by machinery. The days of railroad building were over, and there was less dockyard work because there were fewer cargo boats on the rivers. Many African Americans moved to large cities in the industrial Northeast of the USA.

Many migrating African Americans followed the major train routes north.

They wanted to find jobs and a better standard of living, and hoped to escape the racial discrimination that was common in the South. By 1950, only 20% of African Americans still lived in the Southern states.

This huge migration of people changed the social and economic structure of America. It was one of the important factors in the growth of blues as a major form of popular music.

City entertainment

Many migrants to the big cities faced new hardships, which were mainly caused by overcrowding and poverty.

A group of musicians play the blues outside a run-down apartment block.

These tough conditions produced a new type of blues, known as city blues. City blues was a more aggressive style than country blues. It was often played by larger groups, with instruments such as saxophone or trumpet (shown below). Blues became less personal and more structured and arranged, with musicians playing together.

Trumpets were popular in city blues bands, because their sharp, clear tone made them easy to hear in noisy clubs.

Tenor saxophones were also popular for their loud, booming tone.

Chicago

Chicago became the focus of blues during the 1920s and 1930s. A series of duets by the singer Leroy Carr (1905-1935) and the guitarist Scrapper Blackwell (1903-1962) were among the first recorded examples of city blues.

A poster advertising a new record by Leroy Carr

These songs had the personal, expressive feel of country blues, but their melodies were more regular. The rhythms were more insistent and urgent than many country blues records.

Downhome blues

When the United States entered the Second World War in 1941, more and more workers were needed to staff the weapons factories in the northern cities. This encouraged an additional 1.5 million black workers to move north from the South.

Their taste for country blues led to the development of a city style known as "downhome" blues. It was like traditional country blues, but it was louder and more intense. It was usually played on electric instruments. Some of the greatest blues musicians were downhome players, including Muddy Waters (see Star File), Little Walter, and Howling Wolf.

Blues clubs became very popular in all the major American cities.

In the late 1940s there was increasing demand for blues. There were blues clubs and radio stations in all the major cities, and sales of blues records continued to grow.

California and Memphis

Outside Chicago, different blues styles were evolving. In California, a smoother, quieter, more relaxed style was made popular by artists such as T Bone Walker.

In Memphis, blues radio stations and the record industry made blues very popular. One Memphis DJ became the most important post-war blues musician, B. B. King (see Star File).

A DJ playing blues records that reach an ever widening audience

BIG BILL BROONZY

Big Bill Broonzy (William Lee Conley Broonzy, 1893-1958) grew up on a farm in Arkansas, before settling in Chicago in 1920. There he learned to play the guitar with a light, lilting syle. In the 1930s he became a leading figure among blues guitarists and vocalists, providing music that people could dance to.

Broonzy toured Europe in the 1950s. His hits include *John Henry* (1951) and *Black, Brown and White* (1951), a protest song.

MUDDY WATERS

Muddy Waters (McKinley Morganfield, 1915-1983) was one of the most important post-war blues singers. He started playing blues in Mississippi.

In 1943 he moved to Chicago and began to record. He successfully adapted the bottleneck style to the amplified guitar, using a slide. Touring extensively, he was later particularly popular with white audiences. His recordings include *I'm your Hoochie Coochie Man* (1953) and *Got my Mojo Working* (1956).

B.B. KING

Probably the best known blues singer of any period is B.B. King (Riley King, b.1925). His initials stand for "Blues Boy". He worked in Memphis as a DJ and made his first record in 1949. He taught himself to play the guitar. King performed with a mixture of speech and song. In the 1960s, he became the idol of British rock musicians such as Eric Clapton and Mick Jagger. His album "There Must Be a Better World Somewhere" won a Grammy Award in 1981.

After Midnight

Playing this tune

If you have an electronic keyboard, *After Midnight* would sound good played using the "jazz organ" setting. If you are playing it on a piano, make the chords in the left hand sound very rich and sustained. Make the quavers very relaxed - count carefully, but do not rush.

More playing hints

First, learn *After Midnight* without worrying about the words. When you can play it well, try singing at the same time, or ask someone else to join in.

A blues singer would probably make some of the notes in this tune into blue notes, by singing them a little higher than they sound on the keyboard. Try this with the first E flat in bar 8 and the B flat in bars 13 and 25.

In many blues songs, one of the musicians, such as a guitarist or keyboard player, improvises a solo part in the middle. This often lasts for the first eight bars of the 12-bar progression, and the singer joins in again for the last four bars. Bars 17 to 24 of this tune are written to sound like this type of solo, but you could improvise your own. Make it last eight bars.

The Runaround

Playing this tune

This tune will sound best as a piano solo. Practise the rhythms carefully, and try to make the chords even and firm. In bar 12, play the first semiquaver with the second finger of your right hand, and the next note with the second finger of your left. Alternate between the two.

New harmonies

Some of the harmonies in *The Runaround* do not strictly belong to a traditional blues scale. But the chord progression itself is a minor-key version of the standard 12-bar format. In the 1950s and 1960s, blues continued to grow and develop as new musicians used blues progressions as the basis for all kinds of improvisation.

More about improvising

The second half of this tune is written to sound like an improvisation. The rhythmic and melodic ideas in the right hand here could form the basis of your own improvisation. You could play the tune several times, improvising a different right-hand part each time you play the second half. The last time through, play the coda to finish.

Playing this tune

If you find the syncopated rhythm of the bass line tricky,
first play it without the tie. Then, when you add the tie, try
to keep the beat steady. Practise the left hand until you can
play it automatically, without thinking about it. Then add
the right hand, taking care with the syncopations.

Blues Today

In the late 1950s the audience for blues began to decline, as other types of music became popular with African Americans. Many blues performers found they could no longer sell large numbers of records in the face of competition from new styles of music like rock-and-roll. However interest in blues increased among young white audiences, particularly students, both in America and Europe. This encouraged blues artists like B. B. King, Son House and John Lee Hooker to tour American universities, where they attracted large audiences. As people began to investigate the roots of rock-and-roll, they realized that it had developed from blues. This led new audiences to discover blues, so it remained popular. Many rock musicians of the 1960s were heavily influenced by blues.

Rock-and-roll star Elvis Presley

Guitar stars

In the 1970s there was a fashion in blues for instrumental solos by "guitar stars". These musicians include Albert King (1923-1992), Freddy King (1934-1976) and

Blues performers were popular in American universities

Albert Collins (1932-1993). In Chicago, several performers adapted B. B. King's guitar style to Chicago blues, calling their music "West Side Soul". Magic Sam led the field in the development of this fast-fingered guitar style. He was later followed by Otis Rush, Jimmy Dawkins and Magic Slim.

Modern blues

Artists who have come to prominence since the late 1980s include the Texans Kenny Neal (b.1957), Larry Garner and

Sherman Robertson. Lucky Peterson (b.1964), a child prodigy on piano, has since become a talented guitarist.

Rock guitarist Jimi Hendrix (1942-1970) was heavily influenced by the blues.

JOHN LEE HOOKER

STAR FILE

John Lee Hooker (b. 1917) grew up in Mississippi but later moved to Detroit. Particularly adept at combining his voice and his rather limited guitar playing into a single instrument, he is also given to accompanying himself with his tapping foot, to hypnotic effect.

Long recognized as an influential blues figure, in the 1990s he suddenly became a superstar with a series of recordings including *The Healer* (1990) and *Mr. Lucky* (1990).

ROBERT CRAY

STAR FILE

Robert Cray (b.1953) is probably the best-known blues star of the 1980s. He was born at Fort Benning, Georgia and grew up playing jazz and soul before discovering the blues.

A talented singer and guitarist, he formed the Robert Cray Band in 1974. They released their first album, *Who's Been Talking*, in 1980. Their pure blues style has become increasingly popular.

Cray has regularly played with Eric Clapton, Keith Richards, B.B. King, and Chuck Berry.

Listening to Blues

If you have enjoyed the music in this book, try listening to some of the famous blues musicians mentioned in it. This will expand your knowledge of blues and its history. If you are familiar with some of its most famous records, it will help you to play blues well. The recordings in this list can be obtained from any good record store.

About Blues

Legends of the Blues, Columbia (Roots N' Blues) CK46215 (US), 467245-2 (Europe)

The Roots of Robert Johnson, Yazoo CD1073

The Origins of Blues

Sinners and Saints, Document DOCD5106

The Roots of the Blues, New World 80-25-2

The First Blues

Mance Lipscomb: *Texas Songster*, Arhoolie ARHCD306

Ida Cox: *Blues for Rampart Street*, Original Jazz Classics OJCCD1758-2

W.C. Handy's Memphis Blues Band: Memphis Archives MA7006

Leadbelly: *King of the 12-String Guitar*, Columbia (Roots N' Blues) CK46776 (US), 467893-2 (Europe)

Recording the Blues

Ma Rainey: *Ma Rainey's Black Bottom*, Yazoo CD1071

Bessie Smith: *Complete Collection*, vols.1-4, Columbia (Roots N' Blues) C2K47091, C2K47471, C2K47474, C2K52838 (US); 467895-2, 468767-2, 472189-2, 472934-2 (Europe)

Blues Instruments

Mississippi Sheiks: *Complete Recorded Works in Chronological Order, vol. 1 (1930)*, Document DOCD5083

Gus Cannon & his Jug Stompers: *The Complete Recordings*, Yazoo CD1082/83

Clifford Hayes & the Louisville Jug Bands, Volume 2 1926-1927, RST Jazz Perspectives JPCD1502-2

Charley Patton: *Complete Recorded Works in Chronological Order*, Document DOCD-5009/5010/5011

Memphis Minnie: *Hoodoo Lady*, Columbia (Roots N' Blues) CK46775 (US), 467888-2 (Europe)

Sonny Boy Williamson: *King Biscuit Time*, Arhoolie CD310

Country Blues

Skip James: *Complete Recorded Works in Chronological Order (1931)*, Document DOCD5005

Furry Lewis: *Complete Recorded Works in Chronological Order (1927-1929)*, Document DOCD5004

Blind Blake: *Ragtime Guitar's Foremost Fingerpicker*, Yazoo CD1068

Blind Boy Fuller: *East Coast Piedmont Style*, Columbia (Roots N' Blues) CK46777 (US), 467923-2 (Europe)

Texas Alexander: *Complete Recorded Works in Chronological Order*, Matchbox MBCD-2001/2002/2003

Lightnin' Hopkins: *The Gold Star Sessions, vol.1*, Arhoolie CD330

Robert Johnson: *The Complete Recordings*, Columbia (Roots N' Blues) C2K-462222 (US), 467246-2 (Europe)

Son House and the Great Delta Blues Singers, Document DOCD5002

Blind Lemon Jefferson: *King of the Country Blues*, Yazoo CD1069

Piano Blues

Piano Blues, vol. 1, The Twenties, Story of the Blues CD-3511-2

Boogie Woogie & Barrelhouse Piano, Vol. 1 (1928-1932), Document DOCD5102

Albert Ammons & Meade Lux Lewis: *The First Day*, Blue Note CDP7-98450-2

Jimmy Yancey: *In the Beginning*, Solo Art SACD1

Memphis Slim: *1940-1941*, EPM 15803-2 (French issue)

Blues in the City

Leroy Carr: *Complete Recorded Works In Chronological Order, vol. 1 (1928-1929)*, Document DOCD5134

Little Walter: *The Essential Little Walter*, Chess CHD2-9342

Howling Wolf: *Chess Collectables vol. 2*, Chess CHD2-9349

Elmore James: *The Classic Early Recordings 1951-1956*, Ace ABOXCD2

T-Bone Walker: *The Complete Imperial Recordings 1950-1954*, EMI (Imperial) E22V-96737 (US), CDP7-96737-2 (Europe)

Big Bill Broonzy: *Good Time Tonight*, Columbia (Roots N' Blues) CK46219 (US), 467247-2 (Europe)

Muddy Waters: *The Best of Muddy Waters*, Chess CHD31268

B.B. King: *Live at the Regal*, MCA MCAD31106

Blues Today

Albert King: *I'll Play the Blues for You*, Stax SCD8513-2 (US), CDSX007 (Europe)

Albert Collins (with Robert Cray and Johnny Copeland): *Showdown!* Alligator ALCD4743

Buddy Guy: *The Complete Chess Studio Recordings*, Chess CHD2-933

Magic Sam: *West Side Soul*, Delmark DD615

Otis Rush: *1956-1958 Cobra Recordings*, Flyright FLYCD1 (Europe), Paula PCD1 (US)

Jimmy Dawkins: *All for Business*, Delmark DE634

Magic Slim: *Raw Magic*, Alligator ALCD4728

Larry Garner: *Too Blues*, JSP JSPCD249

Lucky Peterson: *Lucky Strikes*, Alligator ALCD4770

Joe Louis Walker: *Cold is the Night*, Ace CDCHM208

John Lee Hooker: *Blues Brother*, Ace CDCHD405

Robert Cray: *Bad Influence*, Hightone HCD 8001 (US); Mercury 530.245-2 (Europe)

Guitar chords

The diagrams in this box show you how to play the guitar chords used in this book.

C7   D   D7   E♭7   E7   F7   G   G7   A♭7   A7   B♭7   B7

Index

The publishers are grateful to the following organizations for permission to reproduce their material.
Cover Leadbelly - Redferns, London;
p 17 Ida Cox - Max Jones Archive, Sussex; W.C. Handy - Pictorial Press, London; Leadbelly - Pictorial Press, London
p 25 Mamie Smith - Pictorial Press, London; Ma Rainey - Pictorial Press, London; Bessie Smith - Pictorial Press, London
p 33 Charley Patton - Pictorial Press, London; Memphis Minnie - The Weston Collection; Sonny Boy Williamson - Pictorial Press, London
p 41 Robert Johnson - Pictorial Press, London; Son House - Pictorial Press, London; Blind Lemon Jefferson - Pictorial Press, London
p 48 Jimmy Yancey - Pictorial Press, London; Memphis Slim - Pictorial Press, London
p 55 Big Bill Broonzy - Pictorial Press, London; Muddy Waters - Retna, London; B.B. King - Retna, London
p 62 Jimi Hendrix - Retna, London; John Lee Hooker - Redferns, London; Robert Cray - Retna, London